To ma, baba and my sister, the biggest supporters of my passion, the needed critiques of my life and my rock through everything. This wouldn't have been possible without you.

AN EYE THROUGH MY *Kaleidoscope*

MAKE A STORY OF YOUR OWN

DRIKSHITA DAS

Copyright © Drikshita Das 2023
All Rights Reserved.

ISBN 979-8-89002-983-6

This book has been published with all efforts taken to make the material error-free after the consent of the author. However, the author and the publisher do not assume and hereby disclaim any liability to any party for any loss, damage, or disruption caused by errors or omissions, whether such errors or omissions result from negligence, accident, or any other cause.

While every effort has been made to avoid any mistake or omission, this publication is being sold on the condition and understanding that neither the author nor the publishers or printers would be liable in any manner to any person by reason of any mistake or omission in this publication or for any action taken or omitted to be taken or advice rendered or accepted on the basis of this work. For any defect in printing or binding the publishers will be liable only to replace the defective copy by another copy of this work then available.

Contents

Contents

Introduction

I believe every single person on this planet has a story to tell. I mean, just look around.

Try standing in a local train or a crowded metro and keep your ears and eyes open. Just by standing there, you would come across so many stories. The sheer amount is overwhelming! A phone call here, a side glance there; the way someone's hair is made; whether they are wearing a pair of worn out jeans, or crisp formals; the way they are standing; the backpack they are carrying. Hidden in every little detail, there is a story that culminates to lead to the present, the exact moment that you and that stranger, in a totally unaware way, are sharing.

Just a tiny peek into one's life can reveal so much.

But imagine if you could read their minds, learn what they were feeling in that exact moment. Would the stories you just figured still hold true?

Maybe that phone call with the boss that sounded agitated, wasn't like that at all. Maybe the cheesy web series on their phone that your side glance caught wasn't really something they were into but they were still watching it because someone close to them wanted them to. The entire narrative changes. Just because emotions came into play.

An Eye Through My Kaleidoscope is an attempt to recreate that crowded metro, with just one person in focus, but in reverse of what is true for real life. I have given you small peeks into the character's life, through the emotions she is feeling, and left it on you to figure out what is going on in her life. And boy, are these emotions colourful!

So, my dear reader, I hope you weave a story like no other.

Rules to Read the Book

Hold your horses, what do you mean by rules?

When I say rules, I mean rules in the most arbitrary fashion possible.

This book is not just a compilation of various poems and short stories. No.

This book is a single story. It's the story of my life.

But the best part about this story is that it is told without completely being narrated!

Like I mentioned earlier, my intention here is to provide you with not the entire story, but small peeks in the story, how I saw the world and how I felt, and leave it to you to connect the dots.

So, if you really go to see, you are the writer of this story!

As the reader, you are the main character here. I have lent to you the emotions and in some places, certain situations. YOU choose, based on the emotions your character is feeling, what situation he or she must be in. It's on YOU to make sense of it, make a narrative out of it.

You may relate to some of the poems and short stories that follow. You may not relate to others. But what I have strived to give to you is a Kaleidoscope. And when you read each piece, you are sneaking a peek through that Kaleidoscope.

And just like a Kaleidoscope, this book comes in various colours!

The poems and short stories range through a variety of emotions. However, these are emotions that I felt when I wrote them. Since you are the main character in this book, I have left it to you to decide which pieces convey what emotions to you. So, if you are feeling a certain way and want to read something accordingly, all you have to do is look in the index and flip through the pages and voila!

Just like you twist a Kaleidoscope and the colours and design just change.

These poems and short stories span over about seven to eight years of my life. So, if you are a keen observer, you will probably notice a change in the writing style over time. There are time gaps between a few pieces and some others, I have written in a short time. I have tried to arrange the pieces in a way that delivers my growth, as a person and as a writer, through them.

So, the rules of how to read this book are pretty simple.

There are no rules.

If you read it in a chronological manner, a story will unfold.

If you choose to read the pieces in singularity, you'll realise that each piece is in itself, a story.

And if you choose to read as per the emotion that you think it carries, I would like to think that you would be able to relate to them and I can only hope that the happy ones bring you the same comfort they brought me when I wrote them.

Happy reading!!

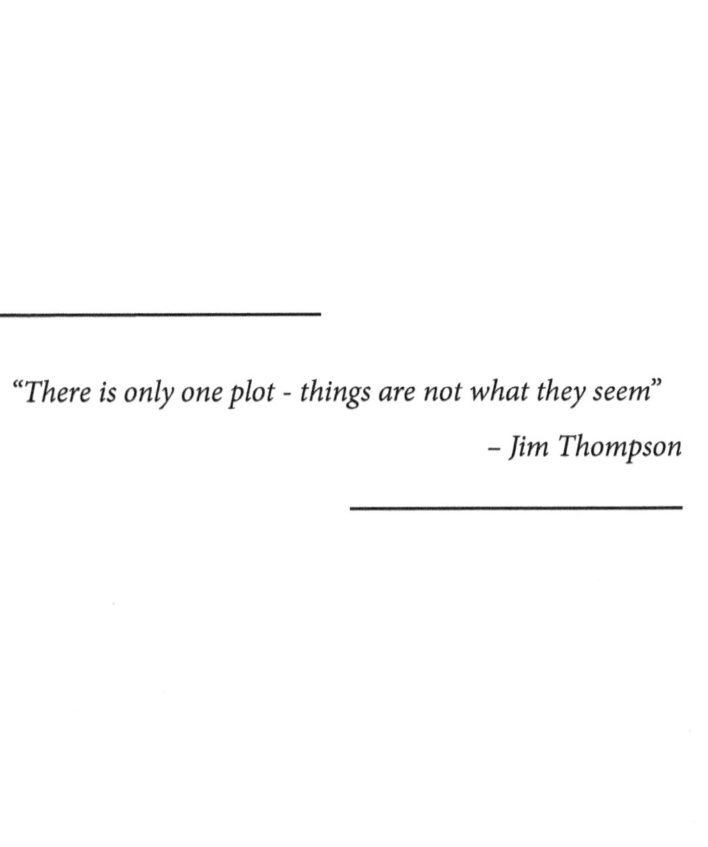

"There is only one plot - things are not what they seem"
– Jim Thompson

A Slit of Memories

I looked at that balcony.

More precisely, stared at it.

From my kitchen's window, diagonally opposite, was the balcony of my neighbouring house. The cobwebs at the corners dangled like a symbol of lack of occupancy and the once white washed walls had after all, started to peel off again. The door's pane was slightly broken, giving me a slit of a view of the inside of that place.

I could barely see anything, but I could remember everything.

We both were the best of friends. Well more like sisters. She used to be at my place all the time or I used to be at hers. Perks of having a bestie live literally two steps away from you, eh?

She was like my breather in this world, someone to whom I could share all my troubles (well what possible trouble could a ten-year-old have? A lost pencil?), I could tell her everything. I could share with her my ugliest fears which, as I grew up, I learnt are called insecurities.

Looking out at that balcony and the microscopic view of the inside of that house, I realised how I remembered every inch of her home; where her study table was, her dressing table's location, every damn thing. Many millions of tiny bits of memories seemed to fly to me from that musty house.

Suddenly the lights went out, snapping me back to reality, the present, and I realised there was a power cut. I turned inside my kitchen again and washed the rice and dumped it into the cooker. As I set the cooker on the gas stove, a faint memory made its way to the front from a long gone time.

When we were kids, I recalled, whenever the power went out like this and the landlines went down, I used to run to my kitchen, grab a stool, stand up on it to reach my kitchen window and simultaneously she too would run to her balcony, and probably, stand on a stool to reach to her balcony railing. And then we continued talking. Because power cuts could never really interrupt that interesting conversation about who screwed up that answer in the classroom.

I smiled. Life had come a long way since then.

Our parents had transferable jobs so at the age of 13, when her father was transferred across the country, my whole life quite literally came crashing down. That was the first time I felt hurt in my life. Real hurt. The type that feels like a thousand pins puncturing your heart and not being able to do anything about it.

We had cried like anything. I still remember. That warm night in the May of 2014. 3 am. The roads of the colony were deserted. I was in my night suit. Ma had woken me up. We had done a Princess Diaries marathon the night before so anyway, we had slept quite late. The cab was waiting, standing there, with suitcases laden on it, like a bulky reminder of the fact that from that day forward, I was supposed to learn to live without the person I grew up with. And then it was time to go. We had just hugged each other and cried our hearts out. It was painful and I didn't even care to hide my feelings. That was something that I learnt a few more years later in my life.

If only time could be lived backwards.

The pain I felt was almost physical that day. All of your life you spend with this person by your side and then one fine day you are left alone. For a teenager like me, it was a pretty devastating feeling.

But we learnt to live on our own.

Both of us.

That's life. You think you won't be able to, but you do it anyway.

All those promises of talking regularly and keeping in touch are being kept, virtually. From talking every day, to once a month, to big moments, to just the birthdays, our lives didn't let us completely keep the promises we had made. It is a truth of life that as we moved away, maybe we moved apart as well. But that's just how things work sometimes. Because the reality is, time doesn't reel backwards, it only rolls forward.

It's been ten years and the last I had seen her was on a mobile screen nearly two years ago, her face distorted with pixels.

At times, I still miss her a lot, yes I do. Although after she left, I learnt independence, but still there are many times in life where I wished for her to be there by my side. To be here and to listen to me without judging me.

Ankita, I miss you.

But believe me or not, at times I wish you were here, still with me in that neighbouring house, maybe talking from the balcony.

And this time, we wouldn't have needed stools anymore.

Walls

They say walls have ears
don't they know I have a mouth too
and two eyes and a nose
and teeth and toes,
everything a human knows.

With those two ears and those two eyes,
I look at what resides inside
and to this day I count
it's been fifteen years,
I have seen this family
go from tears to cheers!

When they came, I still recall
their kids were little and they had some furniture, that's all.
The relatives and grandparents, they all came in
and it hurt when they drilled holes in me
to hang the photo of grandpa with a flower garland on it.
To see that he won't be around anymore to hold the kids
fondly by their chin.
But life moves on
and I saw it in motion,
the kids became teenagers

and apart from their parents,
I had to face those wild emotions!

From banging doors on me
to taking out the frustration of someone else
to crying in the comfort of my arms,
knowing that I only have ears
and no voice.
So I'll not give you the unnecessary advice,
and let you weep peacefully
right under my eyes.

And it seemed like
the cruel clock hated me,
age started showing on me.
The girls grew old,
the parents' hair started turning grey
life is a not a concrete plan,
and it was about time that I learnt that
it'll have its own way.

One fine day, I saw the furniture moving,
they were being packed
in cartons, tight and compact.
My family was moving out.
I was shocked and sad.
But I knew that was that.
There was so much dust and chaos,
but I enjoyed it,

I knew all of this
was my life's last ounce.

One week later, everything was gone,
there remained the four of them looking around,
at me and the tiles,
and through the windows outside
for the very last time,
I saw their faces
which, in my heart, had found very precious places.

Yes I have a heart.
Are you surprised?
I am too.
Because later that night,
looking at the dark inside
I had tears in those old eyes.

Wick-Tim

A little back story:

During the first year of my college, an advocate had visited the college to give a seminar on laws relating to women's safety. My friends and I had, to be very honest, opted to attend the seminar for the sole reason that we would get a legitimate reason to bunk. But as the seminar progressed, that advocate managed to keep us hooked.

There was this one thing she had said that just somehow, stuck with me, affected me, almost hurt me. This poem is a product of that.

He lay there.
A dark figure on the dark ground,
wearing a dark hat and a dark shirt
and crying his dark soul out,
for mercy from the silhouette standing in front of his eyes,
in desperation, spilling out all his life's lies.

I looked at him through my bandages
and tilted my head a little on the side,
he looked just like me,
when I begged him not to strip me off of my pride.

But did he listen?
Well that's a pretty rhetorical question.

I bent down and tore his shirt and pant
and his screams filled the sky
I didn't muffle them up,
because I knew those screams would very soon die.
Just like mine did.

His naked body glistened
with the grace of the moonlit sky.
I stepped on the middle of his body,
he screamed, and I don't know why,
But *I* was the one who had tears in her eyes.

I pushed and pulled and threw him
up and down,
exactly like he had thrown me around.
My bandages had ripped
and blood was all around,
I tortured him till he didn't make a single sound.

He lay there, amongst the bushes
and I felt horrible
I don't know how he lived
with a burden, so unbearable.
But he was breathing,
so I knew he was still alive.

And the deal was to settle the accounts.
I was already dead. So he inevitably had to die.

I grabbed an axe that was kept aside.
On the clink of metal, he fearfully looked at me, upright.
"Oh no please no!", his voice quivered.
"Wh-who are you?", his mouth shuddered.

"Me?" I gave a hysterical laugh,
"I am Nirbhayaa and I am Bhanwari Devi,
I am **every** woman who is abused and raped
because **YOU** wouldn't stop at anything"

And with that, I swung the axe down.
Blood spilled as a blood curdling scream filled the clouds.
And then with the axe in one hand,
I turned around,
dragging the bloody axe on the ground.

I killed a rapist and not a man,
because, as it is often misunderstood,
the man isn't the problem.
The problem is the rapist
and a rapist is an agender monster in and out.

I walked out of the bushes with ripped bandages and teary
eyes.
But out of nowhere, a smile suddenly on my face,
came by.

I am a victim who can earn her own dime.
I am a victim who turned wicked with time.

I, am no more just a victim
Honey, I am now a **wic**ked vic**tim**.

And I am coming.

Freeze

Photos.

Aren't they the easiest way of freezing time?

Well, perhaps the only way.

Take a gander at this one, for example.

In my hand, I hold an old dusty photo of my mom, beaming at the camera, my sister and I, kissing our Nani on each cheek, and she, hugging us.

It was Mother's Day, I remember. Nani and Nana were visiting us. For all the years till me and my sister couldn't afford to buy gifts with our own money, Mother's Day quintessentially meant either a handmade card, or a silver foil covered photo frame (the guy in Art Attack was my idol, LOL) or just about anything that we could make with whatever we found lying around in the house.

This time, there were two mothers in the house.

My sister and I made two drawings of something I cannot remember now and wrote 'Happy Mother's Day' on top of both.

Baba got two pastries because "a big cake is just one flavour" and we put candles on them and both the mothers blew it.

We gave them both the cards and gave Nani a big, warm kiss on each cheek and she hugged us tightly, not even realising that right in that second, Nana was taking our picture.

Today, after years, I look at that photo and somehow, I have time travelled.

Even now, when my Nani is no more, it feels like that memory is etched in eternity. I still get to relive that warmth, that happiness, with just that single photo.

If at all, I would say, photos are underrated.

Because through that one click, my Nani is still alive.
Her smile.
Her warmth.
Her everything.

With just that one photo.

The Valentine Dies

It was early on in the year 2019. As the entire world looked forward to celebrating love on 14th February, all of us received the devastating news of the Pulwama Attack that killed 40 CRPF soldiers of our country. The entire nation was in shock and grief. Suddenly the entire social media that was already covered in red changed its hue to a deeper, darker red, the colour of blood.

Just like other people, it affected me too. Thoughts went on in my head as I read stories of the families of the martyred. And it got me thinking, is there ever really a winner in a war?

The red roses bled
as the entire country wept
over the shards of flesh
that were once our soldiers.

Black, this day has become dark.
as each one of us shed a tear
not because of a heartbreak
but because today, this heart aches.

One moment the sky is blue and happy
and the other moment, its painted black
with smoke and dust of explosives
eating lives, so so corrosive.

As I scroll down my news feed
I find myself constantly be asking
why the war? why the bloodshed?
will we all stop, when we are all dead?
Think about it yourself
We all keep fighting in the name of revenge.
If this goes on,
will the wars ever end?

This question keeps on tossing in my head
as I toss around the rose in my hand
a real tear rolls down
as I lay the rose on the ground
and light a candle and keep it down
with the thousands of people who came out
to show their love and respect
to the heroes of our country in every aspect.

My Valentine's rose lay amongst the many other roses on
the ground
making an ocean of red,
which earlier today would have symbolized romance
but now made up for a sea of despondence and death.
Who knew even the roses wept?

Inside A Train Compartment

It's so weird to travel from Kolkata to anywhere without my family. Sitting on the side-lower berth of the train, I look at the family right next to me.

The kids shouting and jumping around, the mother all flustered on them for being so difficult and their father, quietly, laying the white IRCTC sheets, making their beds. I smile as I realise it is exactly how my family was years ago when me and my sister were kids.

I remember how baba used to get us all excited when the train took a turn. Didi and I would run to the window to stick our faces as far as possible against the window glasses and watch the train's tail. He was the one who taught us why train journeys were beautiful. The vivid landscapes, diverse people inside as well as outside the train and let's not forget, weak network coverage. We talked about all the small villages that passed us in a blur and how their lives were so different from ours. When I was even younger and our train happened to be stuck on a long signal waiting, baba would tell me to give a push to the train. And believe it or not, sometimes the train actually started moving! I remember beaming about being so immensely strong!

And it was also funny how didi and I used to call dibs for who would get to sit on which side of the window. Eating our food not without first cleaning our hands with a hand sanitizer, soap AND a hand sanitizer again. And oh, how ma would shout at us for carelessly touching our dirty feet when we sat with our legs up on the seat! Now when I try to open a ketchup satchel while I eat my breakfast, I miss how ma ALWAYS used to carry a pair of scissors, just in case. Baba remembered almost all the stations on our 2000km journey from east to west.

We were (and still are) workaholics. Those 26 hours were the family time we all desperately required. All those long conversations that started from how the economy is going down and drifted to why I hadn't finished my summer holidays' homework yet are the ones that I miss now.

And today, as I sit alone on this train, sticking my face on the window glass to look at the train turn, I smile.

Baba would have counted the boggies too.

Everything is Lost

Stale breath and a sweaty head,
masked-up and one hundred percent
living my greatest dread,
looking for a bed,
frantically running
but finally finding
a bed and an oxygen cylinder,
who knew breathing would
become such a wager?

In the background of
ambulance sirens and wails of pain,
its difficult to smile
at your loved ones lying on the bed
possibly suffering in vain.

But you have to.
And so I did.

And then again, there I was
stale breath and a sweaty head,
masked-up and one hundred percent
living my greatest dread,

watching him struggle and
unable to do a shred,
I watched him fight for his last breath,
and just like that he went.

It is difficult to process that sudden void,
that sudden blow.

But you have to.
And so I did.

But a flat-line and a hospital bill,
One human life's reminisce, is that it?
In the crematorium that same day,
I stood there watching the flames
that burnt what was humanly left of him.
Staring silently,
crying silently,
walking away from the pier
even before it burnt down completely,
picking on an eyelash that fell on my cheek,
putting it on my hand and praying painfully,
to bring him back before he burns down completely,
and then blowing hard on it,
knowing that an eyelash that didn't fly
would not carry your wish to the sky.

But it flew,
and in that instance I knew,

that he was never coming back
never hugging me,
never holding my hand,
and my heart ached
and a tear fell and then another,
as I wallowed in my pain.

The pier had now completely burnt down
and I knew that he was gone.
Everything felt numb and overwhelming.
And in moment,
it is difficult to think that you can soldier through such
times,
that time will demand you to be strong and brave,
that you are not to blame,
that your life, to you, is fair.

But you have to.
And so, I did.

And so, I did.

P.S. The eyelash still flies.

Journey to Hell

A little back story:

The lockdown was a time when the mind wandered A LOT. News wasn't particularly sunshine and rose petals and it was slowly becoming too much. So, I started looking for distractions. There was an online competition and the prompt was 'Describe what you think the journey to hell would look like'.

This poem is how I pictured it to be.

(P.S., Shows and the movies I had watched back then inspired me a lot in various ways)

Open. Close. Open.
My eyes stared emptily,
in an empty dark,
looking for a little spark,
trying to recollect my last memory,
suddenly remembering,
that I was declared dead in a dispensary!

Jolting to its reality,
frantically moving around,
I knew I was in Hell,

but where were the demons,
that we were all taught about?

Then suddenly,
out of nowhere,
I saw a wooden chair,
and on that chair I saw,
a man in his forties,
having cigarettes as if they were candies,
a starkly handsome guy,
with a glass of whisky by his side.

From around his chair,
I saw a cripple of light flair,
and soon enough,
that dark incalculable space,
painted itself into my residence!
cracks in the walls,
furniture that was clearly
intended for bigger halls,
wooden floors with a dent,
oh yes, this was definitely my apartment!

From the corner of my eye,
I saw my mother,
a bewitching brown shade,
her eyes carried lies
that she loved my father to the
moon and skies.

Amidst the smoke and misery,
sitting in the wooden chair my father,
stared stolidly,
at the whisky glass he just emptied,
as if waiting for an impending disaster,
as if wanting to slow time so that he could run faster.
My mother watched, and walked down to him,
asking him what was worrying him,
and in that second
he grabbed her wrist,
and threw her on the ground in a whiff.

Scared, she looked up from the floor,
but he was not in his senses anymore,
He got up from his chair,
and pulled her by the hair,
screaming, she begged for mercy in pain,
all of that hitting the wall and going in vain,
knowing that this would be one of those nights,
when her body would be etched with blue and black lines.

He yanked her like a chain
and bumped her head on the wall,
the cracks bled,
and she gasped like she was almost dead.
My father, red with rage, in his abusive and drunken haze,
grabbed a vase
and aimed it towards her face,
a bell of urgency rang inside of me,

and I sprang and grabbed the bat kept on the bed,
and ran towards him and hit him hard on his head.
The vase fell and clanked on the floor,
my father crumpled in a heap on the ground,
and I stood there,
all alone,
all the sweet memories flashed like it was a movie that was
shown,
"My brave girl" he used to shine,
all of it lying dead with him tonight,
on the dented wooden land,
murdered by his little girl's own hand.

A tear fell and then another,
I killed my father,
to save my mother.

Filled with guilt and remorse,
I threw the bat aside,
but then suddenly,
my father gets up,
goes to the wooden chair,
and has cigarettes as if they were candies,
my mother,
a bewitching brown shade,
her eyes carrying lies
that she loved my father to the
moon and skies,
walks to him,

asking him what was worrying him,
and in that second
he grabs her wrist,
and throws her on the ground in a whiff,
and I stand there wondering
what the hell is happening?

And then I see it.
He grabbed her again by her wrist and
threw her to the ground,
and bumped her head on the wall,
the cracks bled,
and she again gasped like she was almost dead.
Again, a bell of urgency rang inside of me,
and I hit him with my bat in a leap,
and again he crumpled like a heap.
Those memories flashed again,
I was labelled a murderer, again.

I stood there for a second,
and then I realised,
my hell was in my mind,
playing what I feel guilty about,
several times!

My father got up again,
and again sat in his chair,
I had only one thing in my mind to bare,
I now knew why there were no demons

ready to roast me in fires,
because guilt is what hell actually desires.

There is and never was any journey *TO* hell,
because, the truth is,
the infinite journey *IS* hell.

My Cherished

A little back story:

When you are kids to parents with transferable jobs, you get pretty accustomed to discarding things with every move. On a broad whole, your life becomes a lot about discarding old things to make place for new things. But that doesn't make letting go of the memories that are associated with those things any easier.

This poem is inspired from that part of my life.

When I was a kid,
I used to HATE letting go of things,
toys, clothes, books,
people.
I remember the night my parents
told me that we would be shifting,
I cried all night in my bed,
curled up, clutching my doll,
soaking her with my sorrows.

A year later, my parents said,
they are giving away my dolls,
I slept alone in my bed that night,

my dolls sitting in a plastic bag
kept aside,
I was preparing myself
for the empty side of my bed
with which, I would have to sleep
from tomorrow night.
But I couldn't, so I stacked my
little storybooks all over that side,
just to fill that empty void.
That night too I cried,
but didn't soak up anyone this time.

A few years passed,
and I grew fond of my books,
the pages told me stories,
ranging from dragons and ponies,
when kids my age used to HATE books,
I would look at them, stacked up or lying loose,
puzzling over which one I should choose.
They shaped my world as I saw it.

And then again,
one night,
my parents told me,
it's time to say goodbye,
"Its too much luggage", they said,
"We would be donating them".

That night, in my room,
I looked at them, stolidly,
how could they do this to me?
I didn't cry at all this time.

The next morning,
we went to the orphanage
and went to the person in charge.
Just as we were talking,
I saw a kid, sitting in a small hall,
and in her hand, I saw my little doll!
She was putting her to sleep,
just like I used to.
She even kissed her goodnight,
just like I used to.

A calm feeling settled in my chest,
I smiled, and kept all my books,
on the library's desk.

They shaped my world,
gave me joy and kept me company,
when I thought I didn't have any,
now it was time,
I shared what I had,
when they can make a person smile,
then why limit it to just mine?

As we sat in the car to leave,
the kids waved and shouted
joyful goodbyes,
I waved at them and smiled,
as I realised that I now finally know,
that it doesn't have to hurt to let go.

In the Name of God

A little backstory:

It was the third month of the first lockdown. Half of the world had started adjusting to this new lifestyle of "Everything-from-home" while the other half still held out hope of restoring their older lifestyles back.

Amidst what already felt chaotic, globally everywhere we could see a lot of religious and political unrest.

One such unrest sparked this poem.

I stand in the dark
of my room, looking out
of the window,
the sky, on fire,
a stark yellow and a hellish orange,
poured scarcely inside.
Flames, red and just as orange,
burnt someone in the middle
of the road,
she was screaming,
blood curdling shrieks,

but her screams were overshadowed,
by the clinks of,
knives and bomb blasts.

In the background of
a sky, red and thirsty for blood,
flames raining down from the clouds,
I saw,
two groups of people,
standing on either of her side,
one side, wearing Kufis and Hijab,
the other, chanting the name of Shiva.
Eccentrically different,
but they still had one thing in common,
their eyes, blazing,
hatred, pouring out of their mouths,
never stopping to listen,
what the other wanted to talk about.

Someone shouts and
everybody runs towards each other,
bearing knives and things
that destroy humans,
cutting through each other,
knocking each other out,
bathing in blood,
hunting like hounds.
The white kufis and the
sculptures of Shiva,

lying on the ground,
painted with death,
seemed to cry for help,
begging them to stop.

At the edge of the road,
she still stood still,
ablaze,
looking at her children,
shedding a tear in shame,
breathing her last breaths,
and then dying, still ablaze.

No one stopped a moment
to care for her, to put out the fire,
stomping on her body,
in their crazy wave of insanity,
never realising that ALL of them,
more than humans,
had just murdered Humanity.

Harcèlement

A little back story:

'Harcèlement' is a French word, the literal meaning of which is 'Harassment'. I came across this word during a conversation with my roommate who happened to be studying French in college.

Almost all of us have had bullies at some points in our lives. For the abused, the abuser is a very gigantic character in their lives. It's hard to forget them. But it might not be the same the other way around.

Overtime, most of us tend to push stuff above it, trying to make that needle get lost in the haystack of life. But a rendezvous with the abuser may bring back unresolved trauma.

This poem is a product of that.

On the street one day,
we bumped and our eyes met,
I stared at you and you couldn't get
why I stared, as if you didn't remember me,
but I did;
the same eyes, the same hands, the same grin,

the same grip.
In those sixty seconds,
I travelled back in a tide
to a place where my worst fears reside,
where I locked them tight,
and gulped the keys hoping that they would never see
daylight.
But you! You somehow found them again right?
And there I was,
lying on my school ground,
covered in dust and bruised around
the places that would hurt me
which stayed under my uniform.

I would stay there like that
crying quietly, until all other kids would go,
so that I wouldn't have to see in their eyes,
what I knew was already there;
humour, disregard or at times,
pity.
Some eyes even had empathy.
But no hand ever came to help me.

This happened one day,
then another,
then another,
then another,
and another,
until I stopped counting,

until I stopped crying,
until I stopped feeling.
Over the years,
I had torn this into a million
unsolvable pieces and hoped
that I was never forced
to put those pieces back together.
But on that street on that one damn day,
we bumped and our eyes met,
I stared and you didn't get,
the reason behind that stare,
and picked up the files I had dropped
smiled, and asked,
"Do I know you from somewhere?

Broken Gold

I wonder how come
I never noticed
how your skin, a beautiful hue
of brown shone like gold
in the evening sun,
how your eyes have
unfathomable depths
and I somehow just fell into them,
how your touch your fingers
leave my skin burning
and toes curling
how when your lips kiss mine
it makes my knees wobble,
how your heart craves for
an ear to listen and a shoulder to cry
because yours was a very
broken childhood and
you don't know this but
you sometimes mumble in your sleep
about those haunted memories,
how your hands would just
fit right into mine,
and how you would hold it tight,

how when the dandelions
in the meadows tickled
our bare skins
you would smile like a silly kid,
how, when we make love
amidst the tall grasses
in the forest
right beside our tent
it feels like you are a part of me
residing outside of me,
as if you ignited a fire in me
deep down somewhere in me,
maybe because
until I saw you
sitting on the grass
under a sky full of stars
I didn't realise that even
broken
things
could
be
fucking
beautiful.

Pretty Memories

I landed at the Ranchi airport and walked outside. Right outside, I could easily spot my mom and dad, standing there, craning their necks, looking for me. I smiled. A sense of ease settled in me. It felt like just a moment ago, I was this 21-year old woman travelling solo from Mumbai to Ranchi amid the first wave of Covid-19 but the moment I saw them, I was just my parents' kid.

I was meeting them after a whole year. I was excited. And even though they wore masks, I could tell that they were smiling too. Eyes don't lie, you know.

As I approached them, baba came forward and took the suitcase from my hand and we started walking towards the parking area. Ma asked the same sequence of questions ranging from "How was the flight?" to "*Moti hogayi hai kya tu?*"

A little annoyed because I had indeed put on some weight, but happy nevertheless, we reached the car.

Papa opened the trunk of the car and started putting my stuff in it. My mom was talking to him telling him where to put what.

I stood back and simply looked at them.
It had just been twelve months but something had changed.
Suddenly, their hair seemed whiter than the last time.
And maybe a few more wrinkles perhaps?
Or a thicker pair of spectacles?
Or just the way they looked?
I don't know.

But it was something that told me that they are growing old.

And when you hit that realisation, it's very hard to gulp it.

As kids, we are always used to looking up at our parents as just parents; the people who have the solutions to all our problems, who want nothing but our happiness and have nothing but unconditional love to give.

And while you know their birthday comes every year just as yours does, but theirs is just an excuse for a party and a cake right?

Ma and baba can't grow old.
But as you grow up, you start seeing them as not just your parents, but also as humans.
Humans who make mistakes.
Humans who need love, care and advice.
Humans who, just like you, grow old too.

Baba closed the trunk of the car and we started our journey back home. He talked to me about how my day of journey in this Covid-19 situation was and ma fed me my favourite dish that she had prepared earlier that morning. And I, just like a nine-year old excited kid, told them about everything and happily gobbled the food.

Maybe parents actually never grow old, ha?

Her

After the first wave of Covid-19 subsided a little bit, on my way back to college, I had the chance to revisit my childhood house. And it brought back memories.

She saw her.
In a foggy, cracked mirror of a silent house,
she saw her, a fourteen year old girl,
in the empty room,
sitting naked on the floor, crying
because she could not understand
the girl who cornered her in school at almost every hour,
the girl who became the monster of her nightmares,
the ones she saw in the morning,
the ones which became true.

She saw her again, now, a sixteen year old girl,
in the background,
laying down on the bed,
looking stolidly at the rope that hung
from the fan,
thinking about the galaxies beyond her ceiling
and then sleeping off

with a knife under the cushion and a note in her hand,
a note, crumpled a thousand times,
saying in faded blue ink, 'I give up.'

Now she saw her, a twenty year old girl,
standing in front of a foggy cracked mirror of a silent
house,
keeping the knife and that very same crumpled note on
the ground
and standing up straight,
looking around the empty old house she once called
home,
she saw the twenty year old girl crying and smiling, at the
same time
and whispering,
'I did it.'

She saw her.
She saw herself.

Just the Celebration

Fireworks burst in the sky.
Weird, I thought,
celebrations at this odd hour,
the hour when the roads were quiet,
the wind was quiet,
the sky was draped in clouds
studded with stars,
sound asleep.
What were they celebrating?
The quiet?
the sky?
or the sleep?
I don't know.
Uninspired, I looked back
into my books,
the green and red scribbles,
the red words being important
and the green ones, most important.
But were they indeed the most important
things in the world?

It's weird,
how when someone sees
the clouds,
someone else sees
the silver lining.
You decide who you are
because as it is famously said,
beauty does lie in the eye
of the beholder.
So, tonight
I closed my tired books,
and looked out the window
to see the fireworks,
and to see not the dark night,
but the bright light,
to see, not the reason,
but the celebration.

Down the Ladder

It is truly said that
when you work hard,
success comes and knocks on your door,
but did you know that when failure comes,
it knocks down,
the whole damn door?
Letting everyone know,
that you slipped down a ring on the ladder,
that you couldn't achieve
what you set out to.
It will make you feel
shattered, broken, crippled,
unworthy.

But remember that even broken colours can paint
rainbows,
that even failures can make you go,
farther than you earlier intended,
that no experience goes waste,
that your hard work still counts,
and that you are just as worthy,
and that in reality,

fallen flowers are
just
as
pretty.

Or maybe, even more.

Lop-Sided Earphones

<u>*A little backstory*</u>:

I had just started my Articleship (internship for CA students, if you didn't know) in Mumbai which involved a lot of travelling in public transportation. I had decided to buy myself a pair of earphones from the stipend of the first month I had interned in that firm. And almost as if my old pair of earphones read my mind, one side of that old thing gave way.

And call it a poet's fault but we love to romanticise everything! So, that's what this poem is; a very romanticised version of my broken, lop-sided earphones.

Through my broken lop-sided earphones,

earphones with just one earbud that functions,
I carry two worlds by my side,
one dipped in monotony
and the other, a hue of whichever shade
I want it to be.
From the silent side of my earphones,
the local trains pass by,
women chatter and bicker,
and babies cry.

This world is getting ready for the hustle,
the constant race
to beat,
God knows who
and to achieve God knows what.

On the other side of my earphones,
melancholy takes over
and sings along with a voice
that is only electronically present,
letting me enjoy an intangible company
of an energy,
that is different from the train,
its women, its babies, or its race.
It's a colourful world,
that'll accommodate my mood,
unlike the other side of the earphones
that doesn't give a hoot
about anybody but themselves,
never stopping for a second,
to take a breath and comprehend,
the consequence
of this race with no finish lines.

So, as I travel through places and worlds
with my broken lop-sided earphones,
seemingly closed to the world but not really,
I'll listen to conversations not meant for my ears,

and also to songs that talk about stars,
all at once
and go through two sets of emotions together.

All of this,
just with a pair of
broken, lop-sided earphones.

Indecision

Chaos, a war.
Battles with guns and bombs
lead to bloodshed,
but a battle in the head,
unleashes dreads unsaid.
Because the blood there
doesn't leak out of your veins
but drips down your eyes
in the form of emotions unspoken,
words that could tear flesh apart.

In this war, there are hearts involved,
hearts that are hurt,
not with a gunshot,
but are draped in the ashes
of something whose pier
has already been burnt.

As you speak your mind out,
in a desperate attempt to
let the chaos out,
you see that the more they materialise
into real, concrete words,

the more the chaos engulfs you,
because that chaos, that indecision,
it's in front of you now,
dangling in the air,
concrete. real. undeniable.

So, what do you do?
You ask me?
I don't know.
Well, you shouldn't be surprised because
I breed indecision in my mind,
I am like a bewitching star-studded night,
tempting, beautiful, needing,
but at the same time dark, scary and
terrifying.
Hurting everyone that comes my way.

I am a chaos.
And in my head, I am a wounded soldier,
a soldier, standing in the middle of the field,
looking at both sides,
indecisive of which side she wants to fight for,
and therefore, at the end,
her wounds give in.
She gives in.

No Chaos

There'll be no chaos
for the duration of one entire song.
For the duration of one entire song,
I'll sit on my window sill,
and enjoy what nature has to provide.
I'll sit on my window sill
and enjoy
the wind,
the stars
and the moon
playing hide and seek
in the clouds
and in the clouds
I'll not see the uncertainty of falling
but the certainty of being vague
yet being happy,
and maybe draw a metaphor
between clouds and my future,
and even smile
at a clever quip
that just crossed my mind
but which I'll never let leave my mouth
because some things are better left unsaid.

I'll think about the vagaries of my life,
the vagaries that make me happy
and then circle back to the clouds,
their firmness
but not their vagueness
and definitely not about the
parallel I just drew between
them and my future,
because for the duration of one entire song,
there'll be no chaos
but peace.
Only peace.

Poison

Cuddling with the wind,
standing on the terrace,
embracing the stars,
smoking poison
only to breathe in
and exhale my anxiety,
knowing full well that
in reality
I sleep with my worries,
their warmth being too familiar to me,
like a toxic partner
I want to but just can't let go off,
like a familiar face;
a familiar face I am scared off
but still won't give up on,
because those are the red evil eyes
that I am okay with getting lost into,
because after a day of pretending
to be okay,
my worries are what really
tie together my entire existence.

But I am untangling those threads,
or at least trying to;
I am trying to talk
without words
because my devils don't speak
but they still say to me
that not being able to express any feelings
is in itself a feeling,
that despite exhaling my troubles in smoke,
my partner awaits me in my bed,
tucking me in to sleep
amidst the chaos in my head,
and then kissing my forehead,
knowing full well
that my loyalties are with them
and that while the smoke leaves me
to venture in the wind,
I won't ever leave its side.

But maybe impulsively
write a poem about it
that absolutely doesn't rhyme.

You Are not a Warrior

You are not a warrior
and that's okay.
Let your heart weep,
you don't have to hide in the dark.
Let those scars scream,
the agony of their past.
The world is a beautiful bitch,
and perspectives are to each their own,
so 'beautiful' or 'bitch' are two views
it is up to you what you want to choose.
Run away for a while
from whatever troubles you
lock the doors if you want,
just make sure the locks aren't completely
welded shut, okay?
Have a look around you,
breath the sunlight in,
walk barefoot on the grass if you will,
laugh and leap and jump around.
Because honey remember,
what worries you overpowers you
and ghosts always come to haunt in the dark.
So, let that tear fall and shatter

don't choke up on your own pain my friend,
because the truth is that this unbending heart of yours,
just doesn't want to admit that
sometimes,
you are not a warrior,
and that's okay.

Introspection

There I am,
sitting in my balcony,
watching the skies pouring
and making the earth moist,
letting go of all things,
she had kept in for so long,
between the lightning that
made the night skies bright
and the thunder that tiptoed right behind,
wondering that do actions and thoughts
share the same timid understanding
as lightning and thunder share?

The actions, they just happen,
amidst a friction that tangibly exists,
and then the thoughts, the interpretation, follow,
silently sneaking up on you,
rumbling fiercely in your head,
making you understand the reason
behind those actions.

Because in the clock that I have lived in,
all I have come to realise is that,
thoughts don't always follow actions,
sometimes actions win that race,
and all we are left with,
what we humans like to call
introspection.

That introspection,
flooding your head sometime later,
whence the actions have been done,
and consequences lived,
making you aware of thoughts that actually existed
in the dark quarters of the head,
always there but never making you aware
of their existence,
until after those thoughts, from their dark corners,
instigate actions,
that at that moment don't make sense
consciously,
but are daughters of thoughts
that have already bred themselves
in your head,
running towards the locked door
of your head,
hiding there only till after,
the actions are lived,
and the consequences, suffered.

So if the time gap between
lightening and thunder,
is indeed called introspection,
then so be it.
Because even if there is a time gap,
between the two,
one thing is for sure,
that thunder never fails to
follow lightning,
even though the thunder was
meant to come first of all.
And however frightening the
thunder may seem to you,
brave your heart to see it through,
because its a law of nature,
that only when the lightning
is followed by that impending, roaring
thunder,
is when there is quiet,
silence,
peace.

And just like the night skies,
you can finally let go of things.

Pretence

I stand there in my bathroom mirror,
my clothes hang on the door, tired from the day's work
and pretence,
and I look at my eyes in the mirror,
and they are clearly looking for something,
God knows what,
water pours from the tiny holes on the hand shower in a
sad curve
pitter-pattering on the bathroom floor.

I take the hand shower off of the stand,
and that sad curve hits me,
but it doesn't hurt me.

Cold water trickles down
every crevice of my body,
as if running down to the ground,
in a hurry to leave me,
because even they didn't want to be a part of a body so
scarred,
scars not of blades and needles,
but of hurt and untied ends.

Shivers run down my spine and
prick every hair on my body,
I iron them out with my hands
but it doesn't help
because I am not feeling cold,
but I am feeling weirdly unaware.

Unaware of my emotions,
unaware of my needs,
unaware of the tears that just warmed my face.

I turn off the shower and
pat myself dry,
wrap my being with it,
look in the mirror,
and put on a smile
and leave that unsettling feeling behind,
leaving her there,
wet, uncertain and naked on the bathroom floor,
waiting for me, sitting there.

Because I know that tomorrow when I'll come back,
she'll be there on that very bathroom floor,
and I'll leave the pretence on the outside of that bathroom
door,
and my pretence will be my bodyguard,
never letting anyone know,

that I have a loyal friend, a parasite,
locked up and sitting eagerly,
waiting for me to give her a hand.

And I'll be there,
like a toxic trait,
giving my hand to the monster that awaits.

And one day, she'll eat me whole.

A Glass Full of Rain

A glass full of rain,
a sky pouring whiskey,
warmth of a cigarette burning to cease
from existence; a typical Saturday night.

I hold a book,
the words of which swirl in front of my eyes,
but still make sense,
so I keep on reading
in between the lines like I always do
trying to figure out the unsaid things
like how weird are black holes,
why were wars ever created,
or why being lost sometimes feels like the only way
to find a way,
why does solace cost more
with time,
and how silence pierces ears sometimes.

As I sip from my glass,
I breathe the rain, its newness but more so its gloom,

pouring like that, crying mercilessly
onto the barren land,
as if wanting to stop, but not being able to.

Hundreds of thoughts swivel
in my head and I wonder,
why is it needed that I learn the price of gain,
by enduring gain,
why most of us feel eroded
from the inside,
yet choose to portray a complete form,
why are wounds, mental or otherwise,
such big attention seekers,
ensuring that we feel pain, know of their existence until
they,
on their own volition,
heal
and become scars
on our existence.

And I keep on reading between the lines,
but suddenly realise that I haven't turned a single page,
but have been staring into a star-less sky,
that's pouring whiskey,
and I sit there, sipping rain.
Knowing, and dare not manifesting,
that if the glass goes empty,
and I start
watching the rain pouring and

pouring the whiskey into the glass,
my mind will go into overdrive
and create a dark yet vivid chaos.

A chaos where these lines go farther apart,
making way for thoughts of the 'in between',
and in all of that,
I'll be standing in the middle of those lines,
holding on to each, trying with all my strength,
to prevent them from drifting.

Because I now know well,
that the feeling of not feeling anything
is in itself a feeling,
so if the lines drift farther apart and the whiskey stops
pouring,
I would be left, with feeling, in particular, nothing.

And so my mind will take,
the only thing it has got; the chaos,
and rip the 'dark' and 'vivid' out
and leave behind only the chaos.
And in it, I know that I will most definitely be lost.

And this time, there may not be a way out.

Ghosts of the Past

"Come here", he tugged at her hand
and pulled her closer.
Out on a walk on a lonesome street,
except for the few stray dogs
and the fewer raindrops, almost asleep,
they walked hand in hand,
their steps in unison
but thoughts astray,
"What are you thinking?" she asked,
looking at him, his eyes wandering
the known roads but lost in them,
he said, "I can't see you in pain, not like this",
"Graves of the past are always dug on soils
that have hardened, so they are meant to be
hard to dig.."
"Let me get an extra shovel, so that I can lend a hand"
"Trust me, with you, I'll always stand".

Silently she listened to him,
clutching his hand tighter to make herself feel,
the reality of his existence by her side,
dwelling in the silence,
she continued her timid stride.

Moments later, she stopped in
her trail,
"Why, why would you want to carry
a baggage whose label doesn't carry your name?"
He took a second, avoiding
looking at her directly, and said,
"Not all things come from a reason that words can convey".

They started walking again,
slowly,
the dark night, as if taking mercy on them,
stopped raining on them.

In their silence, they crossed a tree,
that adorned itself with flowers,
pretty and pink,
he tugged at her hand and ceased her walk,
"I always think of you whenever I cross this block"
"The flowers, they remind me of you"
and with that, timidly he plucked a flower,
pushed her hair behind her ear,
and placed that flower there,
"Pretty, delicate, yet hard enough to weather a storm,
whose strength, she is mostly unaware"

She smiled.
And they continued walking
the night street,

sighing with relief because all of a sudden,
she knew,
that in the darkness of the night,
she found her knight in a shining armour,
wielding not a sword,
but a shovel.

What the November – Part 1

At the age of 23, I realised just how DIFFICULT it is to find a decent place to live in the city that never sleeps. Mumbai is famous for its population concentration so, not getting a house to stay probably checks out.

It all started at the end of the month of October, with my birthday right around the corner. It was a breezy Saturday morning. My roommates and I were just chilling in my room, taking a break from the week's run-around.

And then the phone rang.

I will not bore you with the details but in that very short and totally 'didn't-see'-that-coming' rendezvous, our landlord basically told us to leave in a month's time.

Obviously, we were all pretty taken aback, shocked even. But we recovered really soon.

Okay, so a house in a month's time.

No biggie.

Oh, but it was a biggie. We just didn't realise it then.

Come November, we all started looking for places, contacting brokers. Morning calls from boyfriends were replaced with "*Madam, yeh ghar 4 baje available hai, dekhne aaoge aaj?*" In between office meetings, general life drama, visits to TONS of houses and the ticking clock of our one month's notice period, we just BARELY managed to keep our sanity intact.

Another side story to this whole November chaos was that I wasn't really in Mumbai during this time. My elder sister was getting married in that month so I had to leave for home in about five days after our landlord dropped the bomb on us. I could take a month's break only because I was in between jobs at the time and going home was long overdue. Since I had no idea if we would even be here by the time I came back to Mumbai, I had no other choice but to pack up ALL my shit in two days' time and single-handedly shift everything to my sister's place, who happened to live in Mumbai as well, and catch that flight home. It was nuts, if you hadn't guessed that already.

So, while my roommates, amidst their office meetings and everything, went to countless houses throughout the month, I was trying to help them by giving them leads through the brokers I had contacted. The calendar had flipped pages almost as fast as the four of us had flipped, and before we could realise, half the month was already through and we were still flat-less. The situation, as it were, was getting more and more intense.

We had no idea what we would do by the end of the month if we did not get a house. But then, by the end of the third week, almost by fluke, we found a house.

Or so we thought.

What the November – Part 2

A change of scenery.

In the quaint town of Bokaro, Jharkhand, a girl was quietly sipping her black coffee, leaning on the railing of her balcony, looking at the sky that stretched beyond what the eyes could see, and the sun making a rather gorgeous retirement for the day. All seemed peaceful and calm.

Only it was not.

Inside this girl's head, in a stark contrast to the scenery, a storm wreaked havoc. Everything was liquid in her life at that moment and the cliché, 'change is the only constant' didn't seem like such a cliché after all.

Amidst the wedding chaos, not to mention constant calls from brokers, the ambivalence around my job and the thick layer of uncertainty with regards to having a freaking house to live in, my life in the month of November surely felt like I was a character in someone else's story.

Mom, dad and my sister, all the three of them were nose deep in work, sitting late every day. This was on top of the very predicted family drama that is complementary to any Indian wedding. For the last one year, we had been planning the wedding in Kolkata while living in Jharkhand and Mumbai respectively. So, you can only assume how exhausted we already were. What we didn't know was that the real exhaustion, the most major haul, was still pending. From rescheduling trains, re-booking hotel rooms, making hundreds of last minute decisions in relation to the decorations, food, dresses, seating arrangements and innumerable other things, ten days felt like an eternity and a VERY slow paced movie, both at the same time.

By the end of the third week of November, exactly one week before the wedding, while me and my family started towards Kolkata, my roommates video called and gave me a walk-through of the entire house that we had finalised. The apartment was really good and after almost a month's time, we all finally felt relieved.

But our relief was short-lived.

Three days later, with the wedding just 4 days away, my roommates were headed to the apartment to meet with the owner, make the agreement and finally seal the deal. All of us were eagerly looking forward to ending this mayhem.

However, later that night, I got a video call from my roommates. Expecting to hear the good news, I picked up the phone with a smile. But then they told me. Apparently, when they reached the apartment to meet with the owner, the owner informed them that he could not rent out this apartment as of now due to personal reasons.

And there it was.

If '*perro talle zameen nikalna*' could happen in reality, it would have happened to us right at that second. And it would have been a long, metaphorical but still very much real, free fall from our current 7th floor apartment.

We were staring at each other for a minute.

And then, we all started laughing!!

All of us were SO done. SO exhausted. We were uncontrollably laughing!

After our short-lived laughter attack, we all took deep breaths.

We had just a week left.

Just. One. Week.

It was "*aar-ya-paar*" in which case, "*aar*" basically meant being homeless.

4 days passed.

On the morning of my sister's mehendi, on 26th of November, my roommates called me and told me that they had gotten a house! It was a 3BHK, but we were only four people. The broker had told us that he would find the 5th girl by the end of the month and then the five of us would move in together at the start of December.

I felt relieved, yet again.

I enjoyed my sister's wedding that weekend, finally enjoying a weekend without having to wonder what I would say to the *auto vaale bhaiya* when he asked "*kaha jaana hai?*" at the Mumbai Airport.

After the marriage ended on 28th of November, with the month almost about to take its departure, I took my flight back to Mumbai on the 29th with the warm feeling that FINALLY things were at least BEGINNING to settle down.

The next two days would prove me SO wrong.

What the November – Part 3

I was carrying about 3kgs above the permitted flight-baggage limits. So, on an overall basis, the check-in interaction at the Kolkata airport was a very anxious affair. My security check was no picnic either.

The entire schedule of the wedding was not at all chill. With a timeline as tightly knit as two very, VERY clingy lovers who just won't let go, I hardly had any time to properly pack. Not to mention the fact that I was wearing EVERYTHING that I could possibly wear (and not look too silly) just so that I didn't have to pack it.

Upon landing in Mumbai, I took an auto home.

I rang the bell and stood there, smiling. I was happy to be back. But what I didn't realise was that in about ten seconds, chaos would rein on me.

I was greeted with one of my roommates shouting on the phone.

I went in and sat quietly. I was super puzzled but I figured it was in my best interests to keep quiet until at least the call ends.

After the call, my roommates told me that the last deal we made, for the 3BHK, was falling apart even though we had already given the token money to book the house. Apparently, the broker was now telling us that finding a 5th girl was not possible by him in such a short span of time and that till the time he finds that 5th girl, we would have to pay the rent for the whole of the apartment which was exorbitantly higher than our budget.

We were all lost.

We were sitting on 29th November and we were, for the second time in one week, flat-less.

And in about less than 48 hours, we would be homeless too.

Time was ticking so we figured that the only rational thing to do was to start looking for other places too. So, within two hours of me landing in Mumbai, I was out again, scouting Mumbai for houses. We were like mice following cheese trails put out by brokers, seeing about five to six houses that day, revisiting a few old leads, following a few new ones. And God forbid, if that would go smoothly!

The four of us were exhausted, sitting on the footpath and sipping on small paper cups of chai from a small *tapri*. When suddenly, one of my roommates got a call from one of the many brokers we had contacted over the past month and in fact, who had shown us a few houses earlier that day itself. We assumed that he was calling us regarding a fresh lead. The moment we picked up his call, he started shouting. And he wouldn't stop!

Apparently, he got news that we had visited a house through some other broker when he was the one who had told us about the house first. And boy, was he pissed! So, pissed that he went on to threaten us, warning us about the consequences of what would happen if we did not take this house through him and only him.

We just cut the call.

The four of us were already drained. In every way, shape or form.

Suddenly, we became characters from 'Life in a Metro' where everything else was a blur, people were just passing by, and we were there, sitting on the footpath. Our brains had stopped working.

We somehow calmed ourselves down, said that that broker would not REALLY do anything and geared up to visit the next house on the list.

After travelling from one end to another, we returned home at 11PM that night.

Still highly confused, unsatisfied, hopeless, very much spent and to be honest, a little rattled as well, we turned back to the 3BHK brokers and demanded our token money back so that at least funds wouldn't be locked anywhere.

But, of course they didn't agree right away!

It was as if everyone around us was hell bent on giving us a hard time.

The brokers were adamant. They said that we had booked the house by giving the token money and so, the money would be refunded only if something unruly happens.

But bearing the rent of the entire 3BHK would be a very costly affair for us. We fought but then understood that nothing good would come out of shouting on the phone. Not to mention that we weren't really left with much energy after the day we had had.

A few hours before our deadline was officially going to end, we called up the owner of our house and practically begged him to give us just one extra day. He made a scene about how he had lined up a schedule to get the house painted and how giving us one extra day would ruin his schedule but in the end, he agreed.

Later that night, these 3BHK brokers informed us that they somehow got the 5th tenant. They asked us to meet tomorrow to finalise things.

However, further later that night (yes, that night seemed to be unending), we found out that there was still one obstacle remaining; the society committee.

So, a Live and License Agreement (basically a rent agreement) takes about a week's time to be processed. And the society had really strict rules about letting tenants move in only after they had the rent agreement ready. But since our asses were on fire (quite literally) and we couldn't afford to wait for that kind of time, the game plan was to beg the committee chairperson to let us in on the basis of the provisional agreement. Only if that didn't happen, would we get our token money back. Those were the terms.

30th November arrived. And never more did we wish that November had 31 days in it.

We went to the 3BHK, met the 5th girl and the society agreed. Things seemed to go well. It seemed like we had finally broken that chain of the universe serving us with the shittiest people ever.

But (of course, there is a 'but'), just as we were about to register for the agreement, the broker restated the terms of the rent and jacked up the rent. Said that this was what was originally there and whatever else his teammate had told us earlier was not binding as he was a subordinate and not a partner. The thing was, there was a lot of miscommunication among the team of brokers themselves and ultimately, they said that they weren't doing anything wrong so, in no case would our token money be refunded to us.

And that's when all hell broke loose.

All the pent up anger and frustration just flooded out.

What followed was a LOT of screaming, threats of police complaints, misunderstandings and tears of anger.

We were DONE. We left the house in anger because we understood that nothing was going to come out of screaming at them at the top of our voices. Basically we realised that '*Laato ke bhoot baato se nahi maante*'. We had decided to take legal action. But that's a story for another time.

Right across the society, there was a '*Tabela*' [Cow shed]. We were so fatigued at that point that we just didn't care about anything anymore and just sat right there, right outside the damn *Tabela* and had Kulfis. Now when I think back, I wonder how we must have looked; four young women, in jean shorts or sweatpants and plain t-shirts, sitting outside a *Tabela*, sucking on Kulfis, one is in an office meeting and trying to explain to her boss why he could hear cows mooing in the background, the other three, calling just about anyone who would hear them vent, walking up and down.

I remember looking at the cows and thinking, '*Yaar inke paas bhi ghar hai*'.

We were left with only a handful of houses. So, by the time what went on to be the 12th house that we were seeing in the two days, we decided that there was nothing to do. We had to make a decision, even if it meant choosing the best out of the list of the worst houses.

So, we settled. On the less-bad house.

Called the broker at 11:30 PM on 30th November and told him to book the house.

The next morning i.e., on 1st December, with a heavy (and pretty exhausted) heart, we went to the 'less-bad' house, paid everything that was payable and signed the agreement.

What went down the 12 hours was cartons and newspaper and brown tape flying around the house as we hastily packed our entire house and before noon of 2nd December, we locked the doors on our old house and moved into the 'less-bad' house.

I got my stuff from my sister's place the very next day.

What the November, right?

The Last Sunrise Apart

Sunrises are so overrated.
And rightly so.
An early morning, or a late night
call it whatever you decide,
I saw two people, sitting side by side,
not holding hands,
but just looking,
at the sunrise of the
day of their wedding.
They knew that in just a handful of hours,
they won't get to spend
a moment of solitary,
it would be a mix of jolly faces and jolly loud relatives.
So right this second,
they decided to keep mum,
enjoy the first of the many sunrises
that would come,
that they would share in their lives together.
I saw them from a little afar,
just far enough to prevent a ripple
in their stillness,
I stood there for a moment,
gave my heart the time to fill itself

with a sense of calm and content,
decided to capture this moment,
not in a photo but in fewer words that were not so urgent,
and slowly slipped back into my hotel room,
smiling, I finally lay my head on the bed
and got some rest.
Later that night,
while everyone celebrated the wedding
I celebrated that moment,
that moment,
just like a thousand others that I had witnessed,
that just about proved that,
all you really need,
is a person, who would stop in the moment,
to sit with you and watch,
keeping all things aside,
every overrated sunrise.

A New Beginning

31st December, the night of New Year.

The night sky looked oddly clear for a typical Mumbai night. The air was a sweep of fresh breath. There were only two minutes left before the world turned the calendar to another 365 days. Another 365 days that gave everyone fresh days to take up new opportunities, more opportunities to make new mistakes.

Basically, a start fresh, a clean slate.

And while the entire world counted down eagerly to that fresh start, some more enthusiastically than others, I closed my eyes and remembered all the things that I had endured this year.

The heartbreak, the pain, the calm, the happiness, the nerve wrenching nervousness, the guts, the fear, the loneliness, the tears, the guilt, the warmth.

Everything.

And suddenly, the few seconds before the clock struck twelve, everything flashed right in front of my eyes.

It is said that when someone's dying, their entire life flashes in front of them. So, suddenly, the last few seconds of the year felt like a death. A calm, accepted death of all the bad things in this year. As if, these were the last few seconds I would ever think of them. As if this is the last time those memories could ever hurt me.

As if those memories had lived their lives and these are the last moments of their lives.

And then the clock struck twelve.

Everyone celebrated and cheered.

And in that second, I buried what remained of my past and pain, took a relic from those dead bodies as remembrance of the learnings, and pat the shovel on the ground.

And in that honest second, where everyone else celebrated a new start, I celebrated a much awaited ending.

And finally did what I truly couldn't do the entire year;

I really, REALLY let go.

"There is no real ending. It's just a place where you stop the story"

– Frank Herbert

About the Author

I am Drikshita Das and this book, 'An Eye Through My Kaleidoscope' is a dream come true for me. At this point, I am a twenty-three year old Chartered Accountancy (CA) student, residing in the financial hub of the country, Mumbai. Originally from Kolkata, I was brought up in Navi Mumbai and I went to college in Pune where I got my Bachelor's degree.

As you read the last few lines, some of you might be wondering how the hell did this CA-doing Kolkata chick end up writing a book. Let me take you through a little journey.

I had started writing at the age of 10 actually. It started with writing a poem about a classmate I despised and went on to writing about friendship and just about anything that appealed to my imagination. I started enjoying writing so much that I began maintaining a diary. I realised that I could express my emotions much better when I wrote them instead of actually saying them out loud. And so came pages upon pages of day-to-day experiences, crushes, fights, secrets, lies that I spilled in between those pages. But as life caught up with me, other things started consuming more of my time and from writing daily to writing once a week, that habit simply couldn't survive the wear and tear of time.

That's when poems and short stories became my outlet.

I remember the first fictional story that I had ever written. It was a short love story between a deaf boy and a dumb girl. After that, the stories just kept coming. The short stories I wrote derived their emotions from whatever I saw around me. If a certain emotion made me feel a certain way, I would make up a fictional situation either to express it or to just forget about it. Imagination became my comfort cocoon and so whenever an emotion was too much to handle, I would grab a pencil and paper and jot down my cocoon. That was my merry land, a place where I could get lost in the story those words narrated and forget about my own problems.

But as I grew up, things changed. I went to college, away from my home for the first time. I started pursuing Chartered Accountancy. Life took a complete 180 degree turn for me. It wasn't like the change was bad, but yes, it changed my perspective about a lot of the mundane things of life. And very slowly, as the years passed by, the layer of 'fiction' between my poems and my emotions thinned. So, the underlying emotions started to surface more profoundly.

And that's where we are now.

Since the age of 17, I have been published in nearly a dozen co-authored anthologies. In almost all of those books, whenever I was given an option to write a small snippet about myself, I would ALWAYS say "…someday I wish to publish a book of my own, and who knows, maybe ten years from now, you would be in a bookstore, holding a book with my name on it. I mean, really, who knows?…"

I was right. Who knew?:)

A Note of Gratitude

I had been sitting on the manuscript of 'An Eye Through My Kaleidoscope' for more than three years, daydreaming about publishing a book of my own, but being too damn scared of daring to actually do it.

Shivam, you pushed me out of my comfort zone, helped me through the entire process, assured me that my fears were nothing but that, and were a huge support throughout. So, thank you for being there with me. My roommates who have made an appearance in the story, Soumya, Kavita and Vrushali, thank you for telling me that the thought that I was actually scared to do this was ridiculous. My roommates from my college days, Twisha, Tina, Swarangi and Shivani, who were there, reading my work, critiquing it wherever required, actually influencing a lot of the poems and short stories that have made it to the book, giving me confidence when I didn't have it, and basically for standing by my side, thank you. I love you all.

Of course, my parents and my elder sister, to whom I have dedicated this book, like I said, this book wouldn't have existed if it weren't for them. Ma, you have been the backbone of what I am today as a writer. Thank you for encouraging me to always write, despite everything. My elder sister, Chayanika, I know I can count on you always, like I have my entire life and you have always come through. Thank you for everything.

Baba always said "What are you worried about? You dare to dream. I am here."

Immense gratitude.

To my aunt, Gopa, you were the first person ever who told me that I should publish a book of my own. Thank you for being the very first person to see that in me.

To all the people who have been following me on Instagram, some of them for even years now, consistently reading my stories and poems, showering me with love, you guys have no idea how crucial a part those comments and praises played in the journey of this book. Thank you, guys.

The list goes on.

Of course, I cannot put everyone's names here. But if you were ever, in ANY way, a part of my journey as a writer, know that I am extensively grateful to you.

This book is yours.